Copyright © 1999 by Nord-Süd Verlag AG, Gossau Zürich, Switzerland
First published in Switzerland under the title *Mina und Bär*
English translation copyright © 1999 by North-South Books Inc.
All rights reserved.
No part of this book may be reproduced or utilized in any form
or by any means, electronic or mechanical, including photocopying,
recording, or any information storage and retrieval system,
without permission in writing from the publisher.
First published in the United States, Great Britain, Canada,
Australia, and New Zealand in 1999 by North-South Books,
an imprint of Nord-Süd Verlag AG, Gossau Zürich, Switzerland.
Distributed in the United States by North-South Books Inc., New York.
Library of Congress Cataloging-in-Publication Data is available.
A CIP catalogue record for this book is available from The British Library.
ISBN 0-7358-1036-2 (trade binding) 10 9 8 7 6 5 4 3 2 1
ISBN 0-7358-1037-0 (library binding) 10 9 8 7 6 5 4 3 2 1
Printed in Italy
For more information about our books, and the authors and artists
who create them, visit our web site: http://www.northsouth.com

A Michael Neugebauer Book
North-South Books
New York/London

MINA
AND THE BEAR

By Sabine Jörg
Illustrated by Alexander Reichstein
Translated by Charise Neugebauer

M ina longed for a bear...a teddy bear to cuddle and love.

For her birthday she was given a cute stuffed tiger.

At Christmas she got a big stuffed elephant.

And at Easter she received a stuffed yellow chick.

But no teddy bear.

Mina asked her mother if she was ever going to get a teddy bear.

"Oh, Mina," her mother answered. "You have enough cuddly toys!"

Next Mina went to her father to
beg for a teddy bear.
"Don't bother me with such things
when I'm reading!" he growled.

Finally Mina tried pleading with
her aunt Rose.
But in a disapproving tone
Aunt Rose lectured, "Mina, you
shouldn't be such a greedy child."
Finally Mina realized that she was
never going to get a teddy bear.

A short time later Mina became sick.

She didn't laugh or play anymore.

She didn't eat her dinner.

She just lay in bed.

Dr. Rooney came to check on her.

He looked at her throat and took her pulse.

"Strange," he said.

"She doesn't have the flu or chicken pox."

Dr. Rooney was very puzzled. "What in the world could be wrong?"

Mina continued to lie in bed. She felt very tired.

On the third day, Dr. Rooney asked,

"Mina, is there anything you would like?"

Mina pulled on Dr. Rooney's sleeve.

He bent down and she whispered in his ear,

"Please tell me a story."

Dr. Rooney sat down in the old chair next
to Mina's bed.

Gazing out the window, he began:

"When my grandfather was a little bear . . ."

Mina sat up quickly. "How could he be a bear?" she asked. "You're a person!"

"Yes," answered Dr. Rooney. "I *am* a person. But maybe not completely . . ."

And he went on to explain.

"When I was a child, I wanted a teddy bear more than anything else in the whole world. But I never got one. I wanted a teddy bear so badly that I was convinced I must have come from a bear family. Since I'd never met my grandfather, I decided that he was the one who had been a bear."

Mina laughed. "I want a teddy bear more than anything too!"

"Oh, really?" said Dr. Rooney. He ran his finger over his chin thoughtfully, then continued:

Dr. Rooney

When my grandfather
was a little bear

When my grandfather was a little bear, he loved to play hide-and-seek. He and his bear brother and bear sister would run deep into the dark forest and hide. They weren't afraid, because bears are at home in the forest.

They had a lot of fun together. They broke off branches and hid under them. They climbed in trees and crept in the undergrowth.

Once my grandfather hid behind an old fir tree. He leaned back against the

tree and made himself comfortable. And guess what he saw? Big, ripe

blueberries. He smelled them greedily and then began to pick them. He

stuffed the berries in his mouth and noisily smacked his lips. He enjoyed

the berries so much that he forgot all about his bear brother and bear sister.

It wasn't until nightfall that my grandfather the little bear realized that

they had already gone home. The little bear was all alone. He wasn't afraid.

Well, he tried not to be afraid, and he ran as fast as he could out of the forest.

But in his haste the little bear ran the wrong way. Instead of heading to the

field where his bear den was, he took the path that led to the city of people!

The little bear ran and ran until his paws were sore. He didn't realize his

mistake until the bright lights of the city were right in front of him. The little

bear was too tired to go all the way back. Besides, he was curious. And

everybody knows that curious bears don't sleep!

So the little bear followed the lights into the city. He was amazed by the

houses and the streets, and the shops and squares. So this is how people live,

he thought excitedly. There was a lot for the little bear to discover. Ears

squealed around corners. Women skipped down the street in high-heeled shoes.

But where were the children?

Maybe they're already sleeping, thought the little bear. But at that very moment

a little girl appeared before him. She had long black hair and wore a pretty violet

nightgown. She carried a lacy white pillow under her arm. Taken by surprise, the

little bear didn't move. The little girl smiled and greeted him.

"Hello. I'm Milena," she said.

"What are you doing in the city so late?" the little bear asked.

"What about you? Shouldn't you have gone home a long time ago?" Milena replied.

Then the little bear explained what had happened.

And Milena said, "I dreamed I went for a walk . . . or at least I thought it

was a dream. I woke up here, and there you were!"

As they were standing there together, the night wind whistled by. It blew swiftly through the alleys, nipping at Milena's bare arms and poking at the little bear's fur.

Milena was cold. The little bear was sleepy.

"You know what we could do?" exclaimed Milena. "You could come home with me and sleep on my chair."

The little bear was pleased with this idea. "But tomorrow morning I must go home early," he answered. "Otherwise my parents will be worried."

"Certainly," said Milena. "First thing tomorrow morning you can return to the forest."

So the two went to Milena's house. They quietly tiptoed up to Milena's room.

Milena yawned and crawled into bed. The little bear yawned too and made himself comfortable in Milena's chair. Milena and the little bear were so tired that they immediately fell fast asleep.

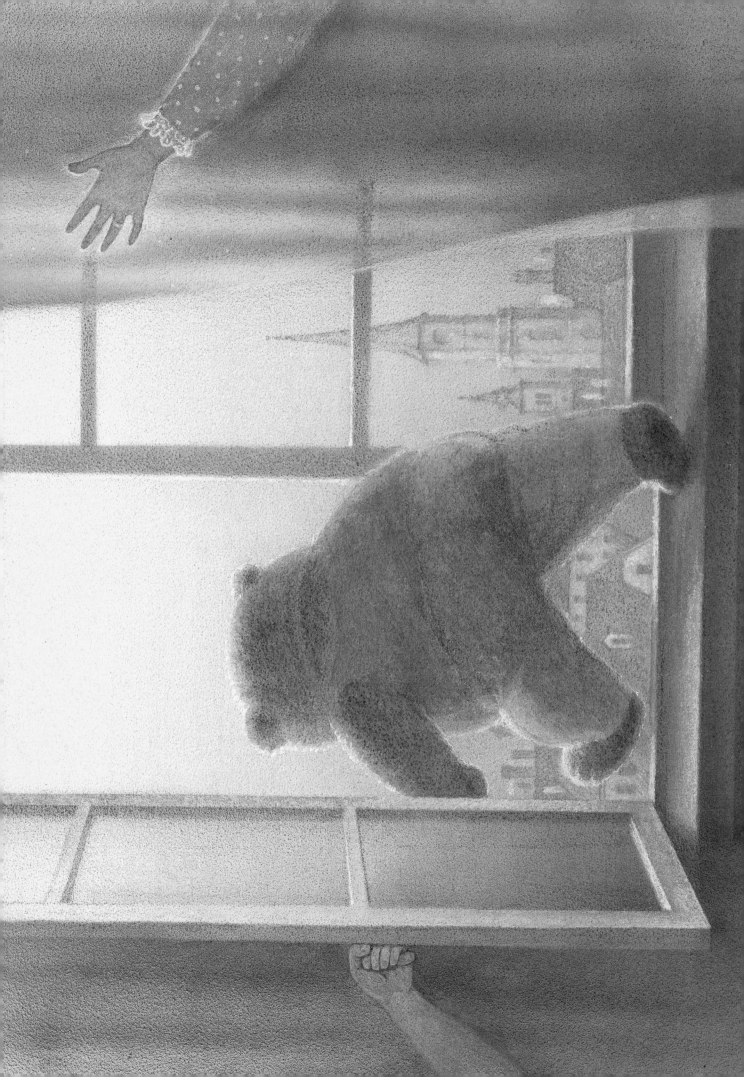

When Milena's mother came into her room the next morning, Milena was still

sound asleep and the little bear was curled up and snoring contentedly.

When Milena's mother saw the little bear, she let out a piercing scream.

Milena and the little bear woke with a start.

"Quick!" shouted Milena as she opened the window.

With one leap the little bear sprang through the window and ran towards the forest.

Milena's mother insisted on knowing how the little bear came to be in

her room. Milena tried to explain, but her mother wasn't satisfied. "Do you expect

me to believe such a story?" she asked.

Milena missed the little bear and the little bear missed Milena.

The years passed but Milena and the bear never forgot each other. The little bear grew taller and Milena blossomed into a young lady.

How and where they found each other isn't known. Only one thing is certain.

They met again.

And one day the little bear, who was then a big bear, married Milena.

My grandfather the big little bear and Milena were the happiest couple anyone could imagine.

Unfortunately, I never met them.

End

At the end of Dr. Rooney's story, Mina didn't look pale anymore. She didn't look tired, either. Mina's eyes sparkled and her cheeks were rosy once more.

"I think I come from a bear family too!" she said, happily jumping out of bed.

Mina's parents thanked Dr. Rooney when they saw that their daughter was healthy again.

Some time later Mina had a birthday.
Mina's mother gave her a stuffed
mama bear in a pretty blue dress.

**Her father gave her
a roly-poly papa bear.**

And Aunt Rose presented her with a
cute little baby bear.
"Thank you," said Mina politely.
"But I really don't need a teddy
bear anymore."

"Who could ever understand this
child?" groaned Mina's mother.

"In my day, children weren't so
spoiled," complained Aunt Rose.

And her father asked, "What would
you like, then?"

"I'd like to have Dr. Rooney come to my birthday party and tell me the story of his grandfather," Mina replied.

So her parents invited Dr. Rooney to the party, and he retold the story of his grandfather the bear. Then he set a basket of blueberries in the middle of the table. "Here, Mina, these are for your birthday," he said. "Just like the ones my grandfather enjoyed so much."
Mina smiled. "You know," she said, "without the blueberries your grandfather never would have met Milena."

Then they all ate birthday cake with blueberries and whipped cream.

"Delicious," mumbled
Aunt Rose, and took
her third piece.

"So healthy," remarked Mina's mother, as she put another spoonful of whipped cream on her berries.

"Not bad," said Mina's father, loudly smacking his lips.

Dr. Rooney smiled at Mina. She smiled back. "It's no wonder we love blueberries so much," she said. "All bears do!"